Kind

A Cherrytree Book

Designed and produced by A S Publishing

First published 1996
by Cherrytree Press Ltd
327 High St
Slough
Berkshire SL1 1TX

First published in paperback 2002
Copyright this edition © Evans Brothers Limited 2002

British Library Cataloguing in Publication Data
Amos, Janine
    Kind - (Viewpoints)
    1. Kindness - Juvenile literature 2. Moral development
    Juvenile literature
    I. Title
    155.4'1825

ISBN 1 84234 149 9

Printed in Spain by G. Z. Printek

Kind

Two stories seen from
two points of view

by Janine Amos
Illustrated by Gwen Green

CHERRYTREE BOOKS

Annie at the seaside

Laura and Annie were staying at the seaside with Annie's mum. Annie was excited. "Two whole days of sea, sand and sunshine!" she sang. She liked being on holiday with her big cousin.

The girls hurried to unpack their things. Then they raced down to the beach. The tide was out. There were great stretches of sand, high cliffs and rock pools.

"Let's go climbing!" called Laura.

"Just be careful, you two!" warned Annie's mum. "Remember, Laura, Annie's younger than you."

"OK!" Laura called back. And off they scrambled over the rocks.

The next morning, Laura and Annie explored the rock pools.

"Look at all the different shells!" said Annie. "Let's start a collection." But Laura wasn't listening. She was watching a girl in the next rock pool. The girl was about Laura's age.

"Got him!" shouted the girl, waving her bucket. "Come and see my crab!"

Annie and Laura ran across. At the bottom of the bucket was a fat, green crab.

"Poor thing!" said Annie.

The girl tossed her head. "I'll put him back afterwards," she said. "I always do."

6

They fished in the rock pools all morning. The girl told them her name was Kate.

"I come here for all my holidays," she said. "I can show you around."

Later, the three girls ran down to the sea. Kate and Laura jumped straight into the waves.

"Let's swim to the big rock! Race you!" called Kate.

Annie knew she couldn't swim that far. She bobbed around in the shallow water. But it wasn't much fun alone.

They had lunch together on the beach. Laura and Kate sat next to each other. They started telling jokes. Annie didn't think they were very funny. And sometimes she didn't understand. But Kate and Laura giggled and giggled.

Annie dug her toes into the sand.

"It's no fun with Kate here," she thought.

After lunch, Kate had an idea. "Let's climb right up the cliff to the café. They sell ice cream." She pulled on her trainers. "It's steep," she told them.

After a while, Annie began to puff. She couldn't go as fast as Laura and Kate. Soon the other two had left her far behind.

Just then, Annie's foot slipped. She held on to the rocks with both hands. A sharp stone dug into her leg, and it started to bleed. Annie wished Laura was with her. Annie's lip wobbled – but she made it to the top.

At the café, Laura and Kate were eating ice cream.
"You've been ages!" said Laura, as Annie came running up.
"You're mean. You don't care about me. I nearly fell!"
shouted Annie. "I'm never coming on holiday with you again."
And Annie burst into tears.

*Read about Laura's
side of things on page 18.*

Tom at camp

"Wow! This is a brilliant tent!" said Tom.

"It sleeps six," said Harry, unpacking his sleeping bag. "I wonder who else will be in with us?"

It was Tom's first Summer Camp. Soon four more boys from his class crawled into the tent with their rucksacks. They were Dan, Nasim, Josh and a new boy called William. There was a scramble and a lot of giggling as all the boys tried to get unpacked. Tom was having a great time.

When they'd unpacked, the boys sat down outside their tents. They waited for their teacher Mr Spicer to speak.

"Here's the plan," he said. "We'll have lunch at twelve o'clock. This afternoon we'll go on our first long walk. Right now, there's a free hour for you to do whatever you like!"

Harry dashed into the tent and brought out a football.

"Let's have a kick around!" he called.

Tom and the others followed him into the next field.

Soon they were chasing after the ball. Harry sent it high into the air – and Tom reached it just in time.

"Brilliant header!" shouted Harry. Tom felt very proud.

After that, the ball went towards William. He missed and it bounced into the mud near the fence.

"Pathetic!" called Harry.

Everyone laughed. And Tom saw William go red. He felt a bit sorry for the new boy, but they were soon chasing after the ball again.

After lunch, the whole class set off on the long walk.

Soon William started to lag behind. He had a blister. Every so often, they all had to wait for him to catch up. No one liked standing around in the hot sun.

"This is boring!" moaned Harry, kicking at a stone.

"William's a real wimp," muttered Josh.

"Wimpy William!" jeered Harry, as William limped along.

Tom looked across at Mr Spicer. But the teacher was too far away to hear.

Dan, Josh and Nasim joined in with Harry.

"Wimpy William!" they called.

Tom saw William turn away.

Just then, Harry grabbed Tom's arm.

"What's the matter with you?" he demanded.

Tom didn't want to get picked on too.

"William the wimp!" he said loudly. But it didn't feel good. Tom knew that William was unhappy.

At last they were back at the tents.

"Have a rest, everyone," said Mr Spicer. "I'm just going to sort out William's foot."

Tom, Harry, Nasim and Josh went into their tent.

"Let's give William a surprise when he comes back!" said Harry. "Let's mess up his things."

Harry shook out William's pajamas and threw them across the tent. Next came his socks. Soon they were whizzing from boy to boy. Tom didn't like the idea, but he wasn't sure what else to do.

"It's only a joke, I suppose," Tom told himself, as he dived after a sock.

At that moment, William came back. Tom thought he looked really upset.

"Those are my things!" shouted William.

Tom collected the socks and handed them to William.

"It's only a game," he said.

"Not to me!" said William in a funny voice. And he ran out of the tent.

Tom felt awful.

For William's point of view, turn to page 24.

Laura at the seaside

Tom and Laura were eating breakfast. Tom was going on a cycling weekend with his friend. And Laura was going to the beach with Aunty Jan and Annie.

"I wish my friend was coming with me," said Laura.

"You've got Annie," said their mum, firmly.

"She's my cousin. That's different!" answered Laura. Laura liked her cousin Annie. But sometimes she wished that Annie was older, especially when they went on holiday.

By the afternoon, Laura, Annie and Aunty Jan had arrived
at the beach. As soon as she could, Laura headed towards the
cliffs. She loved climbing.

"I wonder if I can make it to that ledge?" she thought.
Then she heard Aunty Jan's voice reminding her to take care
of Annie.

Laura sat down to wait.

19

The next morning it was very hot. Laura wanted to swim in the sea. But Annie thought the waves were too big.

"I'd prefer you to stick together," said Aunty Jan.

Laura shrugged. Slowly she followed Annie over to the rock pools.

When they got there, Laura noticed a girl about her own age. The girl was fishing in the water and laughing.

"She looks fun!" thought Laura.

The new girl was called Kate. She was very friendly, and Laura liked her straight away.

After a while, Kate suggested swimming out to a big rock.

"Great!" agreed Laura, though she knew that it was too far for Annie.

"Ready! Steady! Go!" shouted Kate. And she was off. Laura went after her. They were both strong swimmers, and they reached the rock together.

"That was brilliant!" puffed Kate, relaxing on the rock.

Laura screwed up her eyes and peered towards the beach. She could just see Annie.

"She'll be OK," Laura told herself.

After lunch, Laura, Kate and Annie stared at the steep cliffs behind them. Kate knew a way up.

It was a tough climb. Sometimes loose pebbles shot out from under their feet. But Laura thought that made it more fun! She went side by side with Kate until they reached the very top.

Laura felt great after the climb. It was fun to go exploring with a new friend.

Kate grinned at her. "Now let's have an ice cream," she said, pointing to the Cliff Top Café.

Laura and Kate bought their ice creams and flopped down on to a seat. "What shall we do next?" asked Kate.

"We'd better wait for Annie," said Laura, frowning. "I hope she's all right."

Laura licked her ice cream slowly. But Annie still didn't come. Laura began to get worried. Something must have happened. What would Aunty Jan say? Laura felt a bit sick.

Just then, Laura heard someone shouting. It was Annie! Laura was very pleased to see her. Annie came running towards them. And Laura could see that she was cross.

William at camp

William sat in the middle of his bedroom floor. All around him were T-shirts, pullovers and camping gear.

"Don't sit there dreaming!" said William's mum. "You're supposed to be packing for camp."

"I don't think I want to go," said William at last. "I don't know anyone in my class yet. It's horrible being the new boy."

"You'll soon make friends," his mum replied, as she put the rest of William's things into his bag and zipped it up.

William's class set off early the next morning. William had a seat all to himself in the school bus. He looked around at the other boys and wondered whose tent he'd be in. He felt a bit shy.

Soon William was unpacking his camping things, along with Tom, Nasim and the others. William smiled round at them, but they were too busy to notice. He listened to them laughing and joking.

"They're all good friends already," thought William. "I'm the odd one out."

Then Harry suggested a kick around. William didn't like football very much. But he joined in anyway.

Harry and Tom played together for a while. William thought Harry showed off a bit, but he was very good.

Suddenly William saw the ball coming towards him. He panicked. "I'm going to miss, and everyone's watching me!" he thought.

The ball flew straight past. And William heard Harry laughing at him. William felt like running away.

At lunchtime, William didn't feel like talking. He sat on his own to eat his sandwiches.

"Time to start the walk everyone!" called Mr Spicer later. "Pick up your backpacks and off we go!"

"Oh no!" thought William. "I've still got my new trainers on. What if they rub my feet?"

William knew he should change his trainers. But he didn't want to keep people waiting. He didn't want to make a fuss.

"I'll be OK," he told himself, and set off with the others.

After a while, William's feet did start to hurt. He walked more and more slowly. Ahead of him, the other boys had split into groups. They were all laughing and chatting. Soon Mr Spicer came walking back to him. He checked William's feet.

"Blisters!" said the teacher. "Do you think you can make it? I'll ask the others to slow down a bit."

William nodded. He'd made the whole class wait, after all. It felt as if everyone was staring at him.

"I wish I'd never come!" William thought sadly.

Suddenly, William heard his name. It was Tom and the others from his tent. William tried to catch up with them. But then he heard what they were calling, and turned away.

"Wimpy William!" they chanted.

When William got back to the tent later, he was tired and hungry. As he crawled inside, William saw clothes flying everywhere. They were his clothes!

He shouted and the others stopped. But William had had enough. He could feel himself starting to cry, so he ran out of the tent. "I hate camp. And I hate this school!" he thought. "I want to go home!"

Annie says

"Laura's meant to be my friend. We were supposed to do things together on holiday. But she spent all her time with Kate. They weren't very kind to me. They left me out. They didn't even help me up the cliff."

Laura says

"I didn't mean to be unkind. I didn't know how Annie was feeling. I was having such a good time with Kate, I forgot to think about her. Next time, I'll make sure that Annie joins in."

William says

"It's awful being new. You feel left out and lonely. You think everyone is watching you. I tried hard to be friendly and join in. But everyone was unkind to me. I wish I was back at my old school."

Tom says

"It was just a laugh. I didn't mean to be unkind to William. But I didn't want Harry and the others to pick on me. I'm sorry for upsetting William. I could have been friendly to him. I could have helped him to be part of the group."

BEING KIND

Laura and Kate forgot to be kind. They were older and
stronger; they could do things that Annie couldn't do.
They were so busy that they forgot to think of her.
Tom didn't mean to be unkind, either. He knew that
William was feeling unhappy. But he was worried about
standing up to Harry. Sometimes it takes courage to be
kind.
Kindness is about noticing how other people are feeling.
If someone looks lonely or sad, a kind person will help
them to join in. Showing kindness might mean putting
someone else first. That's not always easy. But it's
important to help others feel good. And being kind
always helps you to feel good, too.

*If someone is being unkind to you and making you feel
frightened or unhappy, don't keep it to yourself.
Talk to an adult you can trust, like a parent or a teacher,
or telephone a helpline.
Remember, there is always someone who can help you.*